LET'S TALK...

WRITTEN BY: DR. TARA DOATY-MUNDELL

WITH: HEDDRICK MCBRIDE

ILLUSTRATED BY: HH-PAX

EDITED BY: JILL MCKELLAN

Let's Talk About It

DEDICATION

Understanding childhood experiences goes a long way in our world. This collection of stories highlights the journey to self-discovery that every child travels. It's equally as important to understand and accept ourselves, as it is to be accepted by our families, friends, and the community we live in.

Use these stories as a way to inspire young, brilliant minds to build their self-esteem and confidence. Help everyone realize that coping with difficult feelings is a way to achieve personal growth.

This book is dedicated to my beautiful children and wonderful family. I appreciate your support and encouragement given to me on a daily basis.

ABOUT THE AUTHOR

Dr. Tara Doaty-Mundell holds a Ph.D. in Clinical Psychology from Howard University. She has obtained several certifications in evidenced-based practices aimed at improving parent and child attachment and has over 13 years of experience working with parents and families. Dr. Doaty-Mundell has developed curricula aimed at healing family dynamics and a parenting curriculum, and also one for individuals in recovery from substance abuse.

After receiving her doctoral degree, Dr. Doaty-Mundell worked as the Housing Program Director for Dayspring Programs, Inc., a non-profit agency in Baltimore, Maryland that provides housing and supportive services to families affected by homelessness, substance abuse, and poverty. Dr. Doaty-Mundell stayed in this position until 2012, when she founded Sage Wellness Group, LLC, a consulting firm that provides specialized trainings and workshops for agencies on an array of topics for agency administration, staff, clients and families. She currently has partnerships with corporate businesses, non-profit organizations, churches, hospitals/medical centers, and institutions of higher learning.

Dr. Doaty-Mundell has been the keynote speaker and facilitator of trainings on Mindfulness, Trauma, Parenting, Pain Management, Client Engagement, and Bereavement and currently works as an Adjunct Professor in the Department of Psychology at Notre Dame University of Maryland. She continues to work with families and facilitates parenting groups and a children's Mindfulness group. Dr. Doaty-Mundell serves on the Board of Directors for Mosaic Community Services and on the Advisory Board of The Carpenter's House.

Dr. Doaty-Mundell resides in Baltimore, Maryland with her husband and three children.

There are times when things happen that make me quite sad.
I could have been smiling and then suddenly, I'm mad!

Let's Talk About It

When that happens there is only one way to be.
I have to remember to be mindful of me.

To do this, I will take a breath and not say a word.
I focus on what's happening inside of me, the things that can't
be heard.

Sometimes it isn't easy because I hold onto things really tight.
For some reason those nasty things make me put up a fight.

Then wild things happen and my hair feels on fire.
It's called stress and the feeling is bad, like when my bike gets
a flat tire.

It's times like that which make me see.
I have to always remember to be mindful of me.

Are you wondering what I do when those icky feelings pop into
my mind?
I close my eyes and start to breathe and my thoughts are more
defined.

Other times, I may walk around real slow or move my body
back and forth.

That's when I think about how I have to relax and stay the
course.

I don't want to feel ways that make me feel bad, because the
best things in life happen when I'm positive and glad.

Being mindful of me isn't something that only I should do.
Everyone should do it and that means you, too.

It feels great to calm myself down and stop feeling blue.
It helps me think of others and how all our wishes can come
true!

Everyone can smile and have a happy day.

That's the best way to live and that's what I say.

That's why I always want to remember the power of my inner voice.
When I'm mindful of me, I can make a much better choice.

One of the keys to life is making good choices.

You will be confronted by many bad voices.

People will tell you that it's cool to do bad things.

But you will have to live with the trouble that it brings.

Friends may tell you to steal candy from the store.

You have everything that you need, why would you want more?

Someone may tell you that you should start smoking.

To poison your lungs and ruin your teeth, they must be joking.

They will make you feel bad about getting good grades.

A good report card will help you at any age.

Maybe you should stay out late, and disobey your parents.

That will never work out no matter how you planned it.

You always have to show that your mind is strong.

When you make smart choices, you can't go wrong.

Never do bad things that you don't want to do.

Just to be friends with a group or a crew.

Hang out with people that wish you nothing but the best.

To find them will always be a difficult test.

Find friends that give you some positive thoughts.

They make you think about art, music, and sports.

When you remain positive your mind will be fresher.

Just remember to always fight peer pressure.

Bullies are very small, and I'm not talking about size.

They are missing a few things that can't be seen with our eyes.

Bullies try to target people that they think are weak.

They may tease them or push them around so to speak.

The kids who are picked on may be the ones that are different or alone.

They sometimes are afraid to come outside. They just want to stay home.

Bullies are sometimes the smart and popular kids.

They try hard to make sure that you have no one to play with.

Let's Talk About It

The truth is that they are jealous of something that you have.

So they pick on you in order to make people laugh.

Bullies feel stronger by making others feel small.

They are not that tough after all.

If you are a witness to bullying, stand up for that person.

Being different makes you special, not a target for hurting.

If you are afraid to step in, tell an adult that you trust.

Maybe with a parent or teacher these issues can be discussed.

People are friends with bullies, just so that they can fit in.

Those who stand up to bullies are the ones that will really win.

We should practice treating everyone with the utmost respect.

Then this problem with bullying we will finally correct.

Sometimes it's hard for me to hold my head up high;
There's something really scary about looking someone in the eye.

It's not that I don't want to talk or meet someone new;
Really, it's just that I get tongue tied and don't know what to do.

One thing I do know and I can say for certain;
When you are shy it can be quite the burden.

The good news is that there are some things that I'm trying to
do
In order to make you understand that I really do like you.

A great way to get to know me and see who I am
Is to start talking with me and show you're a friend.

Maybe you could come over to my house and we can do something fun.
We can play with toys, jump, talk, and run.

So what do you say about us trying to be friends?
Once we break the ice, I can assure you that the fun begins.

I can show that I like you and you can show you like me.
It's a great way to start, don't you agree?

I have a protective armor that is wrapped around my mind and heart.
It's there to protect me and now that I have it, I see it's quite smart.

My armor shows others that I feel good about myself.
If somebody says something mean, it doesn't affect my mental health.

I look at them and realize that even if they know me well.
My armor reminds me that I don't need to dwell.

You may be wondering what this armor is and what it's all about.
It's what I call self-esteem and it's so exciting, it makes me want to shout!

Self-esteem is important because it helps me be positive and
strong.
It keeps me smiling even when what others do is wrong.

And what happens when my armor is on is really great!
It shows others that their words and actions are ones I don't
have to take.

They can say something to me that isn't very nice,
But my armor kicks in and becomes my self-esteem protection
device.

Everyone can have armor; it's not just for me.
Parents, teachers, and friends helped me be as strong as can
be.

So now when people ask me to do things I don't want to do,
I can say, "no thank you" and I mean those words—they're
true.

Having self-esteem wasn't always something I had with ease.
However, now it seems more effortless—it's a real breeze.

Through my voice and all my actions, I've learned something
great about me.
When I do the right things my self-esteem grows stronger, like
a mighty oak tree.

⬡ Visit www.mcbridestories.com for more titles.

Let's Talk About It

Made in the USA
Columbia, SC
21 June 2020